imagination vacation

Jami Gigot

Albert Whitman & Company
Chicago, Illinois

I have a very busy family.
Mom works late.
Dad's projects pile up.

Even Marla is always
up to something.

Sometimes everyone is *so* busy,
I really miss them.

"We need a break," I say. "Let's go on vacation!"

Mom smiles.
"I'd love to go to Paris."

"I want to see penguins!"
cries Marla.

"A safari for me," says Dad.
Then he sighs. "Someday
we'll get away, sweetie."

Why wait for someday? I wonder.

I do a little research,

rummage through the closet,

and gather some supplies.

The next morning, we arrive in **PARIS.**
Our first stop is a stylish French bakery.

Marla thinks it looks a lot like our kitchen.
But Mom can tell the difference.
"What a lovely boulangerie." She winks.

Then we view the works of art at the world-famous Louvre Museum.

Mom's favorite is the Mona Lisa.

Dad and Marla prefer newer masterpieces.

Next it's time for a morning stroll.
"Where are we headed?" Mom asks.

I give her a hint.
"It's the most famous avenue
in Paris—maybe even the world."

"Of course! It's the Champs Élysées! I can't believe I didn't recognize it sooner!"

"Imagine all this, just outside our front door," says Dad.
"And look! Is that the Eiffel Tower?"

From the top, we can see
the whole city.

Mom hugs me tight.
"Paris is *magnifique*."

Next we go on **SAFARi.**

I pass out field books and binoculars
so we can observe the native wildlife.

Before long, Dad discovers
a new species!

"I think it's some kind of
monkey!" he calls.

Species: Sam Monkey

Description:
Wears striped tights
Brown hair with
a dash of red

Behavior:
Likes to hang upside
down from trees
Giggles a lot

Diet: Croissants

In the afternoon, we picnic in the tall grass.

Mom has to fend off a
hungry scavenger!

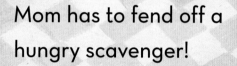

"Ack! A wild hyena!"

After lunch we do some bird-watching.

Dad tells us there are more than
500 kinds of birds in the Serengeti.

"Are there any penguins?" Marla asks.

"Sorry, hon, I think it's too hot for those," Mom says. "But look—a flock of flamingos!"

Marla giggles.

Dad gives me a high-five. "This safari is wild!"

In the evening, we trek across the hot savanna.

"Time to cool down."
I hand everyone hats
and mittens.

OPEN
SKATE
3-7 PM

"But where are we now?" asks Marla.
"This," I announce, "is…"

"antarctica!"

Skate Rentals

EXIT

We step onto the
smooth glacial ice.

"Antarctica is way down
at the South Pole," I explain.
"And it's home to—"

"PENGUINS!" cries Marla.

"They're adorable," laughs Mom.

Finally, we enjoy
the breathtaking view.

"I love it," says Marla, plopping
a warm kiss on my cheek.

"Why don't we go thaw out?"
Dad suggests.

"Oh, Sam, you're tired out from planning our world tour," says Mom. "I think *you* need a break now."

"But we still have to go to
my favorite place," I say.

"Where's that?" asks everyone.

"Home sweet home."

My family is a very busy family, but we always make time for each other.

No matter where our adventures take us.

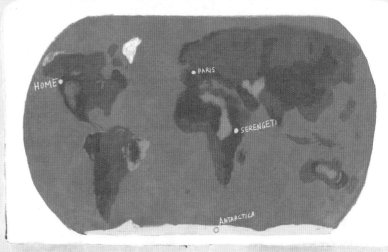

To my very busy family, with love—JG

Library of Congress Cataloging-in-Publication data is on file with the publisher.

Text and illustrations copyright © 2019 by Jami Gigot

First published in the United States of America in 2019 by Albert Whitman & Company

ISBN 978-0-8075-3619-3 (hardcover)

ISBN 978-0-8075-3613-1 (ebook)

Printed in China

10 9 8 7 6 5 4 3 2 1 HH 24 23 22 21 20 19

Design by Aphee Messer

For more information about Albert Whitman & Company,
visit our website at www.albertwhitman.com.

100 Years of Albert Whitman & Company
Celebrate with us in 2019!